Christie Plays Softball

by

Susan O'Hara

Illustrated by Rebecca Barrett

Strategic Book Publishing and Rights Co.

Strategic Book Publishing and Rights Co.
12620 FM 1960, Suite A4-507
Houston, TX 77065
www.sbpra.com

ISBN: 978-1-62516-519-0

"Sweetie, I feel blessed to have the best daughter in the world!"

Other books by Susan O'Hara

Tim's First Baseball Game

Tim's First Soccer Game

"Wake up," (*clap-clap*), "wake up," (*clap-clap*), chirped the Nickelodeon alarm clock.

Christie opened her eyes and looked at the purple alarm clock on her night stand. 7:00!

It was time to get up, get dressed, and get to the game. She smiled and then jumped out of bed!

Today was *her* first softball game, the beginning of *her* softball season, *her* Opening Day. She was so excited*!!*

Christie had started playing baseball when she was 5! As she got older, the girls that had played on her team had stopped playing baseball. They had started to play softball with all of their friends. But, Christie loved baseball! She had always been a baseball player. She loved to run, she loved to hit the ball, and she loved to score!!

But, Christie missed her friends! She finally decided to join her friends and play softball!

When the announcement came to sign up for softball, she and Mom went and signed her up to be part of a softball team! Christie was the first one in line.

They had a practice to meet the coach and the other players on the team. Her team was named the **Blue Wave!** Coach Steve passed out the uniforms. The shirts were blue. Blue was Christie's favorite color.

All of her friends were on her team and she met some new friends too! She knew Leigh, Becky, and Angie. She met Cassie, Jamie, and Madison. The girls had a lot fun together at practice. Christie joined her friends to run around the bases, to catch the ball, and swing the bat.

Christie and Cassie tried on the catcher's gear and caught the balls behind home plate. Coach Steve decided they were both very good at catching, so they would share that position. Both Christie and Cassie played third base too.

Angie was tall and she was good at first base. Leigh did a great job at second base. Jamie was quick, so Coach Steve tried her at shortstop. Madison was a terrific pitcher. Becky was great in center field. What a well-rounded team!

19

So, today was the first game! Christie arrived at the field and joined the rest of the team to warm up. Coach Steve sent Christie to put on the catcher's gear. She was so excited! She was going to catch!

The **Blue Wave** was the home team, so they started out in the field while the other team batted first.

The first batter came up to bat. She swung at the pitch. Strike one! She swung again at the second pitch. Strike two! Again she swung at the ball and missed. Strike three! Christie had caught every ball! One out! Two to go!

The second batter came up to bat. Madison threw the ball. The batter hit the ball and ran to first base, then to second, and then to third. She was safe on third!

Christie looked at the runner on third. She wanted to tag the girl on third base so she didn't run to home plate and score. She looked at Cassie on third. Cassie looked at Christie at home plate. They knew what they had to do.

The next batter came up to the plate. Madison pitched the ball to her. The batter swung at the ball. She hit it! It was going toward Cassie at third base. The runner was off the base and running toward home plate. Cassie threw the ball to Christie at home. Christie reached for the runner and tagged her out! The runner was out! Two outs!

The next batter came up to bat. Strike one! Strike two! The next pitch came right over the plate and she swung! She hit the ball high into the air. Christie looked up. The ball was way over her head. She threw off her mask and put her glove up high in the air. The ball started to come down right into Christie's glove. She caught it!

Three outs!

31

Now it was time for the **Blue Wave** to bat!

Coach Steve showed them the line-up to bat. Cassie was up first. Angie was up second. Leigh was up third. Finally, Christie saw her name on the list. She was the fourth batter.

Cassie stood in the batter's box and took some swings of the bat to warm up. She was ready. The pitcher threw the ball over the plate. Cassie swung and hit the ball toward third base. She ran to first base. Safe!

Angie got up to the plate. She took some swings of the bat to warm up. She was ready. The first pitch was outside. Ball one. The second pitch was outside. Ball two. The third and fourth pitches were outside as well. She walked to first base. Cassie went to second base.

Leigh's turn was next. She took some swings of the bat to warm up. She was ready. At the first pitch she swung and missed. Strike one. She swung at the next pitch and hit it over the first baseman's head. She ran to first. Angie ran to second. Cassie ran to third.

Now it was Christie's turn to bat. She was so excited! She took some swings to warm up. She was ready. The pitcher threw the first ball and Christie swung at it! She hit and it went way over the fence in center field! A home run! Plus, she brought Cassie, Angie, and Leigh home to score as well.

Christie and all her friends had a great time hitting the ball and running the bases. They cheered loudly from the dugout.

The rest of the game was a blur of excitement and the **Blue Wave** won 7-0.

Christie was excited! Christie and her team celebrated after the game and talked over every play.

When it was finally time to leave, Christie found her mom and dad, gathered her equipment and hopped in the car. She said, "That was so much fun! I love softball. Playing with my friends is so much fun! Mom, did you bring my field hockey stick? It's time to get to field hockey practice!"

CPSIA information can be obtained at www.ICGtesting.com
Printed in the USA
BVIW12n2356151217
502935BV00016B/535